A New Home

A New Home

Tim Bowers

Green Light Readers
Harcourt, Inc.

Orlando   Austin   New York   San Diego   London

Matt has a new home.

Matt is sad.
Matt has no friends here.

This is Pam.
Pam has a new hat.

Oh no!
Pam lost the hat.

Matt has the hat.
The hat is here, Pam.

Matt has a new friend!

Pam has a new friend!

Pack Your Suitcase

Pretend it is your moving day.
What special things will you pack?
Make a suitcase to carry them all!

WHAT YOU'LL NEED

construction paper

pipe cleaners

magazines

scissors

crayons

glue

hole punch

1 Fold the paper in half.

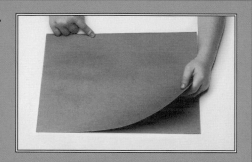

2 Make a handle for each side.

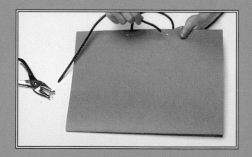

3 Fill your suitcase with pictures.

Ask a friend to guess what is in
your suitcase. Then show and tell
what you have inside!

Meet the Author-Illustrator

Tim Bowers loves writing and illustrating books about friends. To come up with new story ideas, he thinks about his own friends from his hometown in Ohio. He always looks forward to meeting new friends as well!

For information about permission to reproduce selections from this book, please write Permissions, Houghton Mifflin Harcourt Publishing Company 215 Park Avenue South NY NY 10003.

www.hmhco.com

First Green Light Readers edition 2002
Green Light Readers is a trademark of Harcourt, Inc., registered in the United States of America and/or other jurisdictions.

The Library of Congress has cataloged an earlier edition as follows:
Bowers, Tim.
A new home/Tim Bowers.
p. cm.
"Green Light Readers."
Summary: Matt the squirrel has a new home, but misses his old friends.
[1. Squirrels—Fiction. 2. Friendship—Fiction. 3. Moving, Household—Fiction.]
I. Title. II. Series.
PZ7.B6773Ne 2002
[E]—dc21   2001002370
ISBN 978-0-15-204808-2
ISBN 978-0-15-204848-8 (pb)

SCP   15 14 13 12 11
4500488759

Ages 4–6
Grade: 1
Guided Reading Level: D
Reading Recovery Level: 5

Green Light Readers
For the reader who's ready to GO!

"A must-have for any family with a beginning reader."—*Boston Sunday Herald*

"You can't go wrong with adding several copies of these terrific books to your beginning-to-read collection."—*School Library Journal*

"A winner for the beginner."—*Booklist*

Five Tips to Help Your Child Become a Great Reader

1. Get involved. Reading aloud to and with your child is just as important as encouraging your child to read independently.

2. Be curious. Ask questions about what your child is reading.

3. Make reading fun. Allow your child to pick books on subjects that interest her or him.

4. Words are everywhere—not just in books. Practice reading signs, packages, and cereal boxes with your child.

5. Set a good example. Make sure your child sees YOU reading.

Why Green Light Readers Is the Best Series for Your New Reader

● Created exclusively for beginning readers by some of the biggest and brightest names in children's books

● Reinforces the reading skills your child is learning in school

● Encourages children to read—and finish—books by themselves

● Offers extra enrichment through fun, age-appropriate activities unique to each story

● Incorporates characteristics of the Reading Recovery program used by educators

● Developed with Harcourt School Publishers and credentialed educational consultants